# EMMY'S ECZEMA

**Written and illustrated by Jack Hughes**

WINDMILL
BOOKS™

New York

Published in 2015 by Windmill Books, An Imprint of Rosen Publishing
29 East 21st Street, New York, NY 10010

Text and illustrations © Jack Hughes 2012

US Editor: Joshua Shadowens
Editor: Victoria Brooker
Design: Lisa Peacock and Steve Prosser

Library of Congress Cataloging-in-Publication Data

Hughes, Jack, author, illustrator.
 Emmy's eczema / by Jack Hughes.
    pages cm. — (Dinosaur friends)
 Summary: "Emmy has eczema. She knows she shouldn't scratch. But sometimes she just can't
 help it. One day, she scratches so much she makes her skin really sore. Find out how her friends
 make her feel better"— Provided by publisher.
 Includes index.
 ISBN 978-1-4777-9234-6 (library binding) — ISBN 978-1-4777-9235-3 (pbk.) —
 ISBN 978-1-4777-9236-0 (6-pack)
 [1. Eczema—Fiction. 2. Friendship—Fiction. 3. Dinosaurs—Fiction.] I. Title.
 PZ7.H87329Em 2015
 [E]—dc23
                    2013048832

Manufactured in the United States of America

CPSIA Compliance Information: Batch #WS14WM: For Further Information contact Windmill Books, New York, New York at 1-866-478-0556

3 7777 12913 6446

# Contents

Emmy has eczema.

4

This means that sometimes
her skin gets itchy and sore.

Emmy felt a little bit
shy about her eczema.
Occasionally her friends Rex,
Dachy and Steggie would
notice and ask questions.

6

"Does it hurt?" "Is it sore?"
"Can I touch it?" "Will I get eczema now?"
"Of course not, don't be silly," Emmy would
reply grumpily.

7

Emmy knew she should not scratch her skin when it felt itchy. Scratching only made her eczema worse.

SCRATCH! SCRATCH!

8

But sometimes it was very hard to resist.

Emmy's mom made a special cream
out of flowers gathered from the Jurassic
Meadow on the other side of the valley.

Sometimes Emmy complained. "Yuck! I don't like it. It's too sticky!" But the cream did soothe Emmy's eczema and stopped it from itching.

One day, Emmy's mom had run out
of Emmy's special eczema cream.

So she sent Emmy and her friends off to gather flowers from the Jurassic Meadow.

It would take a long time
to get there.

They would need to walk through the forest, cross the river and then climb the Big Hill. As they set off, Emmy noticed that her leg was starting to itch.

By the time they reached the forest Emmy was feeling very itchy. Emmy saw the rough bark of a large tree and before she could stop herself... SCRATCH...SCRATCH...SCRATCH...

SCRATCH!
SCRATCH!

Emmy rubbed her skin against the tree.
"No, Emmy! You MUST NOT SCRATCH!" shouted
Rex. But it was too late. Emmy's skin looked red.

When they reached the bank of the river Emmy felt really itchy. She saw a large rock and before she could stop herself...

SCRATCH!
SCRATCH!

18

SCRATCH...SCRATCH...SCRATCH...
Emmy rubbed her skin against the rock.
"NO, Emmy! You MUST NOT scratch!"
shouted Dachy. But it was too late,
Emmy's skin looked sore.

19

The friends walked upstream to find a shallow place
to cross. Emmy's leg felt itchier than ever. Along the
edge of the riverbank were large scratchy bushes
with spiky red flowers. Emmy could not resist...

SCRATCH...SCRATCH...SCRATCH...
Emmy scratched her skin against the bushes.
"EMMY, NO! STOP SCRATCHING!" her friends
all shouted together. But it was too late. Emmy's
eczema looked very red and sore indeed.

As they crossed the river,
the cold water soothed
Emmy's sore leg.

But as they climbed the hill Emmy's leg became red and sore and itchy again. "Come on everyone, hurry up!" said Rex, "Emmy needs those flowers."

Emmy, Rex, Dachy and Steggie landed, laughing, in a big heap at the bottom of the hill. They were surrounded by the most beautiful flowers.

The friends chased and played. Suddenly Emmy noticed something. "I don't feel itchy anymore!" she said with great relief. "It must be the flowers!" said Rex.

The friends had a wonderful time in the Jurassic Meadow. Rex and Emmy gathered flowers to take home to Emmy's mom.

Steggie made beautiful garlands for them all to wear,
and Dachy flew around chasing the butterflies.

By the time they headed home,
Emmy's eczema felt much better.
Emmy decided she would try really
hard not to scratch her eczema again...

...and maybe her mom's eczema cream wasn't too sticky after all!

# Glossary

**garlands** (GAR-landz)  Circles of flowers or leaves.
**meadow** (MEH-doh)  An area of grassland.
**resist** (ri-ZIST)  To try to keep from doing something that you want to do.
**river** (RIH-ver)  A large natural stream of water that flows into a lake, ocean, or the like.
**sticky** (STI-key)  Coated with a substance tending to stick.
**valley** (VA-lee)  A region of low land that lies between hills or mountains.

# Index

# Further Reading

Close, Edward. *Dinosaur Hunters*. Discovery Education: Discoveries and Inventions.
  New York: PowerKids Press, 2014.

Jeffries, Joyce. *Big and Small*. Dinosaur School. Gareth Stevens, 2013.

# Websites

For web resources related to the subject of this book, go to:
www.windmillbooks.com/weblinks and select this book's title.